P9-EDN-445

Dear Parent:
Your child's love of reading starts here!

Every child learns to read in a different way and at his or her own speed. Some go back and forth between reading levels and read favorite books again and again. Others read through each level in order. You can help your young reader improve and become more confident by encouraging his or her own interests and abilities. From books your child reads with you to the first books he or she reads alone, there are I Can Read Books for every stage of reading:

SHARED READING
Basic language, word repetition, and whimsical illustrations, ideal for sharing with your emergent reader

BEGINNING READING
Short sentences, familiar words, and simple concepts for children eager to read on their own

2 **READING WITH HELP**
Engaging stories, longer sentences, and language play for developing readers

3 **READING ALONE**
Complex plots, challenging vocabulary, and high-interest topics for the independent reader

ADVANCED READING
Short paragraphs, chapters, and exciting themes for the perfect bridge to chapter books

I Can Read Books have introduced children to the joy of reading since 1957. Featuring award-winning authors and illustrators and a fabulous cast of beloved characters, I Can Read Books set the standard for beginning readers.

A lifetime of discovery begins with the magical words **"I Can Read!"**

Visit www.icanread.com for information on enriching your child's reading experience.

Mia and the Girl with a Twirl

www.icanread.com
Book design by Sean Boggs
Library of Congress Catalog Card Number 2012948571
ISBN 978-0-06-208689-1 (trade bdg.)—ISBN 978-0-06-208688-4 (pbk.)

13 14 15 16 17 LP/WOR 10 9 8 7 6 5 4 3 2 ❖ First Edition

Mia and the Girl with a Twirl

by Robin Farley
pictures by Aleksey and Olga Ivanov

HARPER
An Imprint of HarperCollins*Publishers*

There is someone new
in Mia's dance class today.
"Meet Sara," sings Miss
Bird.

Sara looks like a good dancer, Mia thinks.

"Who will show Sara
our dance?" asks Miss Bird.

“We will,” Mia and Ruby say.
They take Sara by the hand.

"Watch us," says Ruby.
Miss Bird plays the music.
Mia and Ruby get into place.

Mia stands on her toes.
Ruby lifts her arms high.
They twirl side by side.

"That looks like fun,"
says Sara.
"Now I will try."

Sara stands in place.
Miss Bird plays
the music again.

Sara does the steps
just like Mia and Ruby.
But she also shakes around!

"What is she doing?"
asks Ruby.

Sara does the moves
while she wiggles and hops.

The dance looks different than what Ruby and Mia showed Sara.

When the music stops,
Sara is beaming.
But the class is very quiet.

"Bravo!" says Miss Bird.
"You move with spirit!"

“I think Sara dances funny,”
Ruby says quietly to Mia.
Mia is not sure what to think.

“Let’s all dance,”
says Miss Bird.
The class gets into place.

The music starts.
Everyone twirls and hops.
Sara wiggles and leaps.

Mia stops spinning.
“Why aren’t you dancing
like us?” she asks Sara.

"I like your steps," says Sara.
"But when I try to do them,
they come out this way."

"But isn't that wrong?"
asks Ruby.
Miss Bird smiles.

"There are many ways
to dance,"
says Miss Bird.

"Learning steps is one way.
Then you can take the steps
and make them new," she says.

Mia gets excited.
“I want to try that,”
she says.

“Me too,” says Ruby.
“Me too,” says Anna.

This time,
when the music starts,
Mia hops in circles.

Ruby starts to gallop.
Bella wiggles her fingers.
Everyone dances in her
own way.

"That was fun!" cries Mia.

The class cheers.

“Thanks for showing us
a new way to dance,”
Mia tells Sara.

Dictionary

Twirl

(you say it like this: twerl) when a dancer spins around

Wiggle

(you say it like this: wi-gull) moving with twists and turns

Bounce

(you say it like this: bownce) short hop or jump

Gallop

(you say it like this: gal-up) a fast run